The Animal Seeker

ISBN-10:1479110558
ISBN-13:978-1479110551

Printed in the USA

The Animal Seeker

Shirley Galbrecht

For my son, Kasen, and my brother, Tommy

CONTENTS

"The clearest way into the universe
is through a forest wilderness."

John Muir

CHAPTER 1

Arcturus

Commander Fike flew his large spacecraft at a low altitude over the surface. Below him, the landscape of Planet Arcturus was empty and barren. Lush plant life had once blanketed the region, but the only remaining signs of life now were a few thorny shrubs. The vast terrain was mostly dry, red clay, crisscrossed by long narrow crevices.

On his right, Fike saw the great city of Marpol. Through the transparent dome that encased it, he noticed countless buildings and structures of every imaginable shape and size. Towering columns connected the city floor to the curved ceiling above. Near the top of the dome, swirling ropes of color and light danced around the tall columns.

Hollow spheres, like bubbles, moved slowly through the air inside the dome. Some were private homes, and others served as transportation, a unique way for Marpol citizens to travel and sightsee. Miles wide, the great city provided shelter for millions of Arcturians. It was surrounded by dozens of miniature domes that enclosed fruit orchards and vegetable gardens to feed the inhabitants.

Fike changed his gaze to look toward the western horizon. There, he spotted two more domed cities,

Javan and Kagu; they were exact replicas of Marpol, only smaller in size.

Fike was beginning a voyage, one that would take him far into space. His mission, if successful, would bring an exciting project to completion. Before leaving the planet, Fike wanted to see firsthand the inspiration for his journey.

The flat plains of Arcturus ended abruptly, and he nosed his ship upward to cross a tall, narrow ridge, red and sharp like the rest of the thirsty landscape. On the other side, Fike saw something glorious, something that hadn't existed on the planet for more than a century. *Is that a…a forest?!*

With wide eyes, Fike looked down on a rich canopy of green as it unrolled beneath him. He marveled at all the hues, shades, and textures. Cutting across the landscape were shimmering lines of blue and silver, rivers snaking through. Here and there, waterfalls could be seen, with frothy clouds of cool, white mist billowing up from the pools they poured into. There were hills and valleys, high cliffs and deep ravines.

There was so much majestic and unexpected beauty there that Fike wasn't sure which way to look. To the left, he admired a meadow of purple and orange flowers, and to the right was a deep lake, so clear that the graceful plants swaying gently in the rippling current could be clearly seen. Arcturus looked exactly the way Oma, his mother's mother, had described it from her memories of the past, a special place indeed.

The lush woodlands covered miles and miles and were the absolute pride of the Arcturians. It had taken many years of patient, difficult work to re-create this wild, magical place.

Fike circled his ship around to take in a more panoramic view of the forest. As he flew above the magnificent wilderness, his mind traveled back in time, to when he was a young boy of nine or ten years old. He could see himself looking at the pictures in his Oma's memory box, peeking at images from the place where his Oma had grown up, outside the domes.

He recalled a picture of a land covered in white, speckled with people standing in the distance, bundled up in colorful robes. They were watching his grandmother, who was only a girl then, and her older brother, Meish.

Oma and Meish were sitting in a cart-like contraption, atop two long, flat runners that seemed to be sliding over the snow. A muscular, four-legged creature covered in thick, curly hair was pulling the cart. It was taller at its front shoulders than at its rear. The creature's face was broad and beautifully sculpted. Its eyes were fire red, focused on the direction they were headed. Oma was holding on to her brother and seemed to be laughing, with a happy, excited expression on her face. Recalling that picture, Fike could almost hear the voice of his grandmother as he recalled her words to him...

"Do you remember what snow is?" asked Oma from behind him, looking over his shoulder at the picture.

"Yes, Oma. You told me all about it, but what kind of creature is this?"

"They were called yomacks. When I was a girl, many people owned them. They were used to pull sleds like the one in the picture, and people also enjoyed their affectionate nature. I had a yomack as a pet."

"Oma, why do we live in the domes now? What happened to the yomacks and all the animals that lived outside?"

His grandmother was quiet for a while; she

walked to a chair and sat down slowly before she spoke. "Arcturus was once a wild and beautiful place, home to many creatures—so many you would not have believed it! Our whole planet was full of lovely natural areas." Oma paused and took a deep breath. "Unfortunately, dear, all that changed. Over time, we seemed to grow more and more interested in our machines and technology. We slowly forgot about our connection to nature. As our technology advanced, our leaders made a decision that it would be better to live inside. The massive domes we live in now were built to shelter our cities, homes, and farms from the elements of nature. Inside the domes, we can completely control the weather and our environment."

"Isn't that a good thing, Oma?" asked the wide-eyed Fike.

"In a way, Fike, I suppose it's very good. For instance, it hasn't rained, snowed, or hailed on us since. We're never too cold or too hot, and we don't have to worry about storms, tornadoes, strong winds, or lightning. Wildlife is no longer a problem because...well, there isn't any. I suppose some would say the domes are almost...perfect."

"Then why do you look so sad?" asked Fike.

"It's difficult to explain to you, Fike. You've never lived out in the open, beyond these transparent walls and ceilings, so you can't possibly imagine what it was like when I was growing up."

"Isn't the outdoors still out there, Oma ?"

"No. Things are very different now. After everyone moved inside the domes, the land outside simply withered and died."

"Why?" asked Fike.

Oma sighed. "It takes great quantities of fresh air, clean water, and rich soil to supply the cities, and all we give back to the outside in return are polluted air, water, and soil. Arcturians have taken many things from the planet, many essential elements, yet we've returned little that is needed to sustain life on the outside," explained Oma.

"What else have we taken from the wilds, Oma?"

"For starters, Fike, we logged the forests for wood, mined the minerals, and drained rivers, lakes, and seas and even melted the snow and ice for water, but we've returned nothing to its original condition. That makes it impossible for anything to survive outside the domes. The animals disappeared so slowly at first that we hardly noticed."

Fike noticed a touch of remorse on Oma's face. "Do you miss living outside?"

"I do now, but at first I didn't mind being inside. Like everyone else, I thought the domes were so much more comfortable than open space. We created many distractions to entertain ourselves, and for a long time, it didn't seem like we were missing anything," replied Oma, "but now I know that we were wrong—very wrong—about that."

"What do you mean, Oma?" Fike asked, wrinkling his brow and trying hard to understand.

"In time, Fike, we grew bored with our domes. We got tired of all the artificial environments and games we had developed to entertain ourselves. We were sick of all of the synthetic, invented things, everything fashioned by Arcturian hands and technology rather than nature. It was then that we realized our catastrophic mistake. We missed the animals, the wilderness, and all the diversity and surprises nature has to offer. Most of all, though, we missed the beauty that had once existed, the natural surroundings that reminded us of who we were and where we'd come from." Oma stood up. "I hope we can turn things around one day—that we can somehow make things right and find a better balance for your generation."

Oma died long before the decision was made to re-create the forest, a decision she would have whole-heartedly supported. It took great effort, but eventually the Arcturians succeeded.

Fike's mind returned to the present. He gazed down at the wonderland beneath him and prayed that his mission would succeed.

There was just one problem with the beautiful woodlands and meadows that the Arcturians had worked so hard to bring back to life: While there was plenty of plant life again, there were no animals, so the forests were almost eerily quiet, lacking the sounds, sights, and wonder of creatures that could move freely through their surroundings.

Thus, Commander Fike, armed with his wits and his memories of a world his Oma had so loved, had been chosen to search the galaxy for planets similar to Arcturus. His mission was to seek out wildlife, capture it, and return the live creatures to his planet. It was hoped that in time, the natural world of Arcturus, outside the domed cities, would once again be thriving and bubbling with life. If the plan worked, a wide variety of creatures would one day fill the forests and future wild places the Arcturians hoped to restore.

A beeping on the instrument panel alerted Fike that it was time for him to leave orbit and begin his journey through the stars. He entered the coordinates that would take him to another world and placed his ship on autopilot, allowing it to navigate him to just where he needed to go.

As he left Arcturus, his home planet, Fike checked his life support systems and began to settle in for a long voyage that he hoped would go faster if he slept through it.

His eyes rested for a moment on the scene outside the window. The light reflecting from the surface of his planet quickly faded as he glided into the deep blackness of space. The star clusters of distant galaxies invited his ship toward their light, and Fike smiled hopefully as he thought about the adventure ahead of him.

He made one final check of his operating systems, closed the hatch cover, and leaned back in his comfortable chair, right in the middle of the control center. In the dimly lit room, computer and navigational screens flickered softly, changing colors and patterns as the instrument panel hummed peacefully, lullabying Fike into a deep sleep in no time.

As Fike dozed, he dreamt of being ten years old again, chatting with his beloved Oma as she showed him pictures of all the feathered, furry, and funny-looking creatures that had once called Arcturus home.

There was the red-horned nesmen, a flying creature with large, scaly wings. It speared its prey with a long, slender horn that grew from the front of its forehead. Its lanky, thin, stalk-like legs were three times the length of its body, and its feet were as agile as hands, equipped with sharp claws.

The beautiful and friendly munzel was a furry animal lined with silver and blue stripes. Its large, hooded eyes made it look sleepy, though it was actually quite alert. It walked on four long legs and held its triangular head high on its gracefully curved neck.

His Oma's favorite was the purple sooge, a long and flexible water-loving animal. The sooge's tail was shaped like a fin to help it navigate through the water. It was very intelligent and full of play and mischief. The sooge had a sticky tongue for catching large insects that flew too close to the water. It would lie just beneath the surface, treading water softly with its wide tail. When a big, juicy bug came along, the sooge would shoot out its long tongue and catch the bug in a flash.

Fike woke from his long sleep with a start to warning sounds coming from the ship navigational system. *Beep-beep-beep!* "Approaching destination. Repeat…approaching destination." *Beep-beep-beep!* "Beginning orbital descent…" *Beep-beep-beep!*

Fike sat up quickly and began touching the controls. He opened the hatch cover to reveal the most beautiful thing he'd ever seen. Absolutely awestruck, his mouth fell open, and his eyes grew into large circles as he gazed at a sparkling blue, green, and white orb floating in space before him. He knew right away what it was, even without looking at the navigation monitor on the console: "Earth! I've reached Planet Earth!"

CHAPTER 2

Tommy's Forest

Tommy was worried. He'd been searching for his dog, Nept (short for Neptune) for half an hour, but the curious canine was nowhere to be found. *That crazy dog,* thought Tommy. *He's always running ahead of me.*

Normally, ten-year-old Tommy wouldn't have been too concerned, as it wasn't unusual for he and his black Labrador, Nept, to find themselves separated in the woods. What worried Tommy was that the night before, Nept had sounded a warning. He had awakened Tommy with all his barking and growling at something outside their bedroom window. Tommy only hoped whatever had startled his dog hadn't gotten a hold of him in some dark corner of the forest.

In the night, they'd both heard strange, unusual sounds coming from the forest, as if all the animals were frightened. Tommy had decided it was best to wait till midmorning to investigate, and the plan was for the two of them to head out together to solve the mystery.

Unfortunately, while Tommy was stocking his backpack with supplies for their forest adventure that morning, Nept had taken off without him. Tommy always liked to prepare for a day spent in the woods. He typically packed his sketchpad and pencils, a peanut butter and jelly sandwich, a water container, a light jacket, and his compass. His supplies varied, depending on what the journey might entail.

Tommy followed Temple Creek, calling out for his dog in exasperation. "Nept? Nept, where are you?" Tommy knew the forest well, and he had every nook and cranny of the areas he'd already traveled perfectly mapped out in his mind. The largest trees grew near the creek. They had remained undisturbed for decades and provided a cool canopy on hot summer days. They also provided homes for many of the forest animals Tommy knew best. Quite the young topographer, he'd drawn maps of the places he and Nept had explored so far, but the forest was large and provided a never-ending source of discovery.

The rolling hills were covered with tall pines and hardwood trees. In the low areas, there were dense thickets of small holly trees, saplings, and shrubs. Huge, moss-covered boulders jutted out of the ground, and rocky bluffs overlooked the river and streams. It was a beautiful place.

"Hmm…that's strange," Tommy thought aloud. "The forest seems unusually quiet today." He didn't hear the familiar chirping of the birds or the chattering of the squirrels, nor did he see the fleeting movements of animals through the trees or any branches rustling, except from the wind. Tommy began to have a very uncomfortable feeling. *Where is Nept, that silly old dog?*

Frowning, he called for his pet and fellow adventurer again. He wanted to find his friend, and he was running out of patience. Something seemed very wrong.

Nept hadn't meant to leave Tommy behind. He'd been sitting on his haunches, waiting patiently outside when one of his favorite pals, Squirrel, caught his attention. Squirrel and Nept often played tricks on each other.

Squirrel was unaware of her surroundings as she nibbled on delicious, fresh buds. When she came within a few feet of Nept, he just couldn't resist such a tempting sight. He sprang to his feet, barking, and lunged after her. The startled squirrel raced into the woods and up a tree.

Squirrel chattered angrily at Nept. "You rascal! That's not funny. Why, you scared the hair off my tail!"

"Come on, Squirrel. Don't be mad. You weren't paying attention," said Nept.

"Wise guy. You just wait. The next joke will be on you!" Squirrel warned as she scurried down the branch and jumped to another tree.

Nept shrugged his shoulders and took a few steps deeper into the woods. He held his nose high in the air and inhaled deeply. *Ah, a perfect spring morning,* he thought. Nept was completely at home in the woods. His short, sleek Labrador coat never got caught on prickly briars and twigs. He was fast and strong and could bound through a tangle of bushes and vines effortlessly.

If Tommy could have experienced the forest through Nept's observant eyes, keen ears, and extremely skillful nose, he would have encountered a very different place. The range of sounds Nept could hear was twice that of his master's; he could hear things four times further away, things Tommy couldn't hear at all, and he could pinpoint their exact location. His sense of smell was 1,000 times better than Tommy's, making the woods an olfactory paradise. The forest that Nept and the other animals experienced was a sensually rich, magical place, filled with information and clues that their human counterparts could never possibly decipher the way they could, in spite of all of mankind's fancy gadgets and gear.

I think I'll say good morning to Fawn, decided Nept. *Tommy will catch up in a bit.* Red Doe often left her new baby in the deerberry and arrowwood thicket while she foraged for food. Nept was used to finding the little guy curled up under one of the bushy shrubs, safe and sound, but on this day, there was no sign of him or his mother. Nept was disappointed but thought little of it. *Maybe Fawn is too old for naps now,* he reasoned.

He followed the deer trail through the thicket to a low area, where the undergrowth was even denser. A hollow area under a fallen tree made a home for Rabbit. Like many of Tommy and Nept's friends, Rabbit was more active at night. "Hey, sleepyhead, wake up!" Nept barked.

There was no response.

"Come out, long ears. I need you to catch me up on last night's happenings."

There was still no answer.

Where is everybody this morning? wondered Nept. *Surely Raccoon will be home,* Nept hoped, becoming more than a little suspicious.

He padded his way down to the creek and

splashed into the stream below a small waterfall. It was deep enough to swim in, and the cold water felt good.

Nept was a natural in the water. He dog-paddled in graceful circles, enjoying himself immensely, then hopped onto a flat, smooth rock. He shook himself dry and paused a moment to enjoy the view.

In the distance, he caught sight of the huge oak tree where Raccoon lived. The long, strong branches reached far across the creek and were covered in brilliant green leaf buds. At the base of its trunk was a cavity large enough to be seen from where Nept stood.

Nept took off running in the direction of the tree, barking a hopeful greeting. "Good morning, Raccoon! It's me, your ol' buddy, Nept!"

Again, silence answered his call.

"Raccoon?" He barked again several times, as if ringing the doorbell. He leaned his head and shoulders into the dark cavity. A shaft of light from a hole above illuminated Raccoon's resting spot, but there was no one sleeping there.

"That's odd," Nept mumbled to himself and backed out of the tree. He thought about the strange sounds he'd heard coming from the woods the night before, then cocked his head to listen more carefully for signs of his friends. He sniffed the ground, hoping to catch Raccoon's scent with his remarkable nose. "A-ha! I've got it." Pleased with himself, he wagged his tail as he followed the scent trail.

Meanwhile, Tommy kept searching for his dog. He'd missed his friend by only a few minutes; in the mud beside the creek, he saw fresh pawprints. *I'd recognize those anywhere,* thought Tommy, used to tracking Nept.

He found a place where he could cross the creek, hopped from stone to stone, and quickly picked up Nept's trail on the other side. When he saw that the tracks led to Raccoon's tree, he called out for both of them. "Nept! Raccoon! Where are you two?" He ran to the big oak but found it empty. Tommy brushed his fingers through his sandy-blond hair and stomped his foot in frustration.

"Nept! Nept!" yelled Tommy. The tracks ended at the tree, and he was stuck on where to go next. "Nept?" He stood motionless, listening, but there was no response.

Nept had followed the scent trail to Big Owl's

daytime roost. It was vacant as well, but the peeps of nestlings were easy enough to hear, coming from nearby. Mother Owl had remained at the nest to care for their chicks, and she poked her head out from a hollow space in the tree where the nest was located.

"Finally, somebody's home!" exclaimed Nept. "Can you tell me what's going on? Where is everyone?"

"I'm not sure, but Raccoon called an emergency meeting at the clearing. You should find Tommy and get down there."

Just then, Nept heard Tommy's voice in the distance: "Nept! Nept!"

"That's Tommy calling now. Thanks, Mother Owl. I have to go."

"Get yourselves to that meeting!" she yelled as Nept raced off. "Sounds mighty important, whatever it is!"

Nept hurried down the hill and met Tommy halfway down. From the look on Tommy's face, he knew he was in trouble.

"Nept, where have you been? I've been looking everywhere for you. Can't you ever wait for me?" Tommy scolded.

The big Lab lowered his head and tail in embarrassment and looked up at Tommy with guilty eyes.

Tommy couldn't bear to see his best friend cower. "It's okay, boy. I was just worried about you. Hey," Tommy said, changing the subject, "have you found out anything about that mystery we're supposed to be solving today? About all those weird noises we heard last night?" Tommy gave Nept an affectionate pat on the head.

Nept quickly resumed his previous excitement and spun around on his hind legs, then took several leaps forward. He stopped suddenly and turned back to face Tommy with an expression of eagerness.

"What is it, boy? You want me to follow you?" asked Tommy.

"Woof! Woof! Woof!" answered Nept in excited barks.

"Okay, boy. You lead the way," said Tommy.

Tommy followed Nept to the clearing. The air was tense and charged with excitement. There was a great gathering of animals there, and all of them seemed to be chattering at once. Raccoon was trying desperately to quiet the crowd but was having no success.

"Wow! What's all this?" wondered Tommy aloud.

He scanned the scene, trying to make sense of such unusual animal behavior. For some strange reason, all the forest animals had gathered there, as if they'd planned it.

Raccoon was going crazy. The frustrated creature paced quickly back and forth, making whistles, trills, and chitters in a futile attempt to capture everyone's attention.

Tommy just stood there with his mouth open, totally baffled.

Nept quickly climbed to an elevated place on top of a huge boulder. "Everyone, may I have your attention please?" he barked.

But no one paid him any. Even when he continued barking, no one listened.

Big Owl decided that Nept needed some help. He flew to a branch above his friend and let out a string of ascending hoots, ending with an ear-piercing succession of short notes.

Suddenly, the crowd was silent.

Tommy was completely amazed. He couldn't imagine what would cause such peculiar behavior. *Do the animals sense a threat of some sort? An earthquake, a forest fire, or some other looming disaster?*

"Thank you," continued Nept in the forest language, which sounded like nothing but a lot of barks, growls, yelps, yips, and whines to Tommy. "Raccoon, Mother Owl told me you called this meeting. What's this all about?"

"Red Doe and Fawn have been captured, that's what!"

All the animals let out a collective gasp.

"It happened last night. I saw it myself," said Raccoon. "They disappeared into this big, strange, flying machine, and now they're nowhere to be found!"

"A big, strange flying machine?" repeated Nept, puzzled.

"Right," answered Raccoon. "There was a bright light shining down from this monstrous flying thing that was hovering in the sky, and it just sort of snatched them up!"

"Was it a helicopter?"

"No, no, no!" answered Raccoon. "It was most certainly not a helicopter. This was more like a, uh…well, kind of flat and—"

"You mean a flying saucer?" asked Nept.

"Yes, exactly!" said Raccoon excitedly. "When that light came down on Red Doe and Fawn, it froze them like statues. Then they started to glow and sparkle. The big ship started humming, and then the light went out, and they were just...gone."

"Let me get this straight. They disappeared into a flying saucer?" repeated Nept.

"Yes!" cried Raccoon, stretching out his hands and arms in exasperation. "A flying saucer, alien space-craft, or whatever you want to call it, flew off into the sky and took them away."

Nept was dumbfounded. He looked at Tommy and wondered how he could ever make him under-stand. Tommy was busy jotting down notes in his sketchbook, which doubled as a journal; he didn't want to forget anything he was seeing, because it was certainly extraordinary, and he was about to find out just how truly extraordinary. Nept hopped down and began barking at Tommy excitedly.

"Hold on, Nept. Let me just write down this last— ouch!" exclaimed Tommy when Nept impatiently nipped Tommy's leg. "Nept! What's gotten into you?" asked Tommy.

Nept continued barking frantically.

Tommy paused and looked thoughtfully at his dog for a moment. Tommy and Nept could almost read each other's minds. Not in a telepathic way, really, but in an intuitive way; they knew one another so well that they could almost guess what one another was thinking.

Something began to click in Tommy's head. He looked out at all the animals for a moment, carefully searching for the ones he and Nept knew especially well and thought of as friends. He saw Raccoon, Big Owl, Rabbit, Beaver and the river otter family. "Who's missing?" Tommy asked.

"Woof!" encouraged Nept.

"Nept, where are Red Doe and Fawn?" asked Tommy. "Are they missing, boy?"

"Woof-woof-woof!" answered Nept, jumping up with each bark. He nudged Tommy with his nose in the direction of the arrowwood patch.

All the animals held their breath in hopeful anticipation, wondering if Tommy would understand. "That's it! Something's happened to Doe and Fawn, hasn't it, boy?"

Nept jumped up and licked Tommy's face.

"All right! All right already, I get it," said Tommy. He wiped his face with his shirtsleeve and thought a moment. "Don't worry, Nept. We'll figure this out."

He gave the anxious dog a reassuring pat. Even though he didn't let on that he was, Tommy was quite worried. He knew Red Doe and Fawn could be in a hundred different kinds of trouble. *Maybe they fell prey to poachers, hunting them out of season, or a predator might have chased them far from home.* There were lots of possibilities, but Tommy decided it was important to stay positive. He looked out beyond the crowd of animals and into the forest. "We'll find them," he said aloud. "There has to be an explanation. Deer just don't disappear into thin air."

But that's exactly what happened, all the animals thought.

CHAPTER 3

First Capture

Fike was delighted with his first capture and couldn't stop marveling at the two lovely animals. They were more beautiful than anything he could have imagined.

The mother and her baby were a good start for his collection, but he knew he'd have to capture more of their kind if the species was going to survive on Planet Arcturus. He imagined small herds of the graceful creatures roaming the forest meadows of his home.

While he was happy to have the deer, his work had only begun, and he would have to obtain many kinds of animals to fill the Arcturian forest with new life. He orbited Earth several times, searching the planet for forests similar to the one the Arcturians had re-created on their planet. While looking for a match, he noticed some disturbing things on Earth's surface.

It appeared that large areas of forest were disappearing from the planet, and patches of it were just gone. Fike was worried that the Earthlings, like the Arcturians, were destroying the natural wonders of their world. He wished he could warn them, but he took some relief in the fact that the few animals he captured would at least be safe and appreciated on his planet.

When Fike discovered Tommy's forest, he was filled with excitement, knowing he'd found a perfect match and was much closer now to fulfilling his mission.

Red Doe and Fawn looked around them. At first, they thought they were still in the woods. They stood on a carpet of green grass with clumps of wild blue violets and yellow lady slippers. There was a small drinking pool at the base of a large rock.

Must be a natural spring, thought Red Doe.

Above, the sky was lit as before, with the full moon and stars occasionally peeking out from behind a thin veil of drifting clouds. Beyond the small meadow where they stood, clusters of appetizing poplar and maple saplings were growing. In the distance, the forest continued, made up mainly of large, old trees and sparse undergrowth.

As similar as it looked to home, Red Doe had the sneaking suspicion that something about their surroundings had changed. Unsure about her location, she walked briskly into the woods with Fawn close behind. Suddenly, she bumped into something hard, an invisible wall. She leapt away, shaking her head in dazed confusion. When she tried to go a slightly different direction, the result was the same. The woods seemed to extend endlessly into the far horizon, but no matter how hard she tried, she couldn't get past the first few trees. Frustrated and baffled, Red Doe bumped up against something solid again and again. "What is this I keep running into?" she asked herself, starting to feel frightened.

The disoriented deer could never have guessed the answer to her question, because never in her deepest imaginations would she have thought that the forest would be surrounded by a force field. The Arcturians had gone to great pains to make their containment areas as natural as possible, but a holding pen could only be so big. If Red Doe could have peered beyond her enclosure, she would have seen a huge hall, the size of a stadium. It was several stories high, seemingly open to the sky. Soon, dozens of similar holding pens would fill the space, as more force fields were activated.

"Don't move!" Red Doe warned Fawn. The distraught deer ran in every direction, trying to break through the transparent wall. When she got nothing but several bumps on the head for her effort, she began to panic, but for the sake of Fawn, she forced herself to calm down. She returned to his side. "It's all right, Fawnie," she said gently, rubbing her nose reassuringly between his ears. "Everything's going to be okay."

Breathing hard, she looked around her immediate surroundings. There was plenty of food and water, and while they'd clearly been uprooted, neither she nor Fawn had been harmed. She didn't understand where they were or how they had arrived in that strange place. The last thing she remembered was a bright light and the feeling that she couldn't move. She decided it was best to stay calm and wait patiently, until some of her questions could be answered. In the meantime, she had a little one to look after.

Fike had been watching from the other side of the force field. He could see Red Doe and Fawn, but they couldn't see him. He breathed a sigh of relief when the mother deer finally relaxed a bit. It troubled him to see her so frightened and confused, for he didn't want them to suffer in any way. He decided it was too risky to show himself to them. Even though he longed to get close, he was afraid his unfamiliar appearance would only upset them more. *Tomorrow or the next day will be soon enough for us to meet. Perhaps they'll rest now*, he thought to himself.

The computer that maintained the deer enclosure also scanned their bodies and checked on their health, then reported to Fike almost everything he needed to know about the creatures. He knew how much water they needed and what kind of food was right for them. He knew what temperature was the most comfortable and how much exercise to provide. The computer even told him if they liked to live in groups or if they were solitary animals. Still, there was much he didn't understand. "Even computers can't know everything about living things," he reasoned.

When the forest below turned away from the sun and into darkness once more, he would try to capture more of their kind, as well as other species. His plan was to obtain enough male and female animals of each species so that they could thrive and multiply when released in the Arcturian forest.

It had been a long night, though, and Commander Fike was exhausted. He headed to his quarters for a few hours of sleep. Quite happy with all he had accomplished, he slept well.

The next morning, he awoke, feeling refreshed. He had a quick breakfast of Arcturian grains and fruit, then started preparations for another hunt. He constructed several more containment areas, but the exact plants, natural features, and environmental conditions would have to wait until he captured more specimens. The deer enclosure was complete, but the computer would have to replicate the surroundings of other animals as he captured them. For the time being, it was enough that the force fields were in place.

He made his way to the command station and took his seat. The instrument panel showed that his craft was functioning at optimum levels. He also tested the transport system, checking to be sure it was working perfectly. The transfer of living matter was tricky business and required precision.

Everything appeared to be ready, but Fike still felt nervous. The importance of the mission was clear to him; above all, he wanted to be successful. He had expected it would take most of the day to prepare for more captures. He checked the time and groaned impatiently, realizing that nightfall in the forest was still hours away.

His thoughts lingered on what his evening might be like. *What amazing creatures will I find? Will I have any trouble catching them? Will the transport go smoothly for me and for them? Are there any potential problems or worst-case scenarios I haven't considered?* Fike was full of anticipation, but he knew he had to wait until most of the lights from neighboring towns had gone out before he could go out hunting again.

To kill time while he waited, he updated the entries in a catalog he was working on, a list of all the animals he had observed so far. It contained a picture of the male and female of each species, as well as information about their habitat and behavior.

He looked out the porthole at the planet below. Despite his restless anticipation, he had a feeling that the hunting would be good that night.

CHAPTER 4

≈≈≈≈

By Accident

The day had started off pleasantly enough, but it was unseasonably hot and muggy. The heat, along with Tommy's restless concern for Red Doe and Fawn, made for an uncomfortable combination. The boy stopped to mop the sweat off his brow and take a cool drink from his canteen.

After learning that Doe and Fawn were missing, Tommy had decided to check everywhere he would normally expect to find them.

Nept reluctantly followed Tommy from point to point, frustrated that he had no way to tell Tommy what he knew about Red Doe and Fawn's disappearance.

"Sorry, boy," said Tommy. "I don't seem to be making much progress, do I? No sign of deer around here."

Nept whined softly in a sympathetic tone and brushed his head against Tommy's hand. The dog knew exactly where the strange disappearance had taken place, because he'd asked Raccoon about it. *If I could just get Tommy to follow me to that spot, we might find some clues.*

Nept suddenly became excited. He barked at Tommy several times and took off at a fast trot.

"Hey! Where are you going, boy?" Tommy yelled after him.

Nept stopped only long enough to turn around and bark at Tommy again, then resumed his course.

"Fine. You lead for a while," said Tommy, as if Nept were giving him a choice.

Once Nept was sure Tommy was behind him, he took off running. He knew the spot Raccoon had described, a grassy knoll not far from the creek, where some young poplar trees were just budding.

The night before, Raccoon had been busy eating some crayfish with his nimble hands when a weird humming noise caught his attention. He hurried to climb a tree to get a better view.

In the sky, he saw a gigantic flying machine, like none he'd ever seen before, hovering with only the slightest movement. Its shape was triangular, with rounded corners; its center was covered in a bull's-eye pattern of circles within circles. Multicolored lights moved like a wave from the outer rim to the innermost circle in a continuous cycle. Near its outside edges were strange markings resembling hieroglyphics.

Raccoon wasn't a brilliant creature, but he was certainly smart enough to know he was not looking at any ordinary aircraft. What he saw next stunned him. The waves of light converged on one central spot, glowing increasingly bright until a sudden burst of light beamed down on the woods below. Caught in that eerie circle of light were Red Doe and Fawn, and that was the last time Raccoon had seen them.

Nept led Tommy right to the spot where he was sure the strange deer-napping had occurred.

"Nept, don't you think it's hot enough without running?" Tommy was soaked with sweat. As he caught his breath, he took a good look around.

On the grassy knoll, where the two deer had stood the night before, a shimmering white substance covered the ground in a perfect circle, forming something like a looking glass.

Tommy approached cautiously and peered into the seemingly liquid pool. As though reflected on the surface of water, Tommy saw the mirror images of Red Doe and Fawn. He looked quickly behind him, expecting to see them standing there, but they were nowhere to be seen. "What in the world?"

asked Tommy.

In response, Nept only growled at the mysterious illusion. Like Tommy, he had no idea what to make of it.

The motionless image of the deer and her baby were still there when Tommy bent down and slowly touched the shimmering pool with his finger. The moment he touched it, it began to swirl and dissolve. In a moment, it was gone. Tommy turned to Nept in confusion. "Did you see that?" he asked.

"Woof!" replied Nept, indicating that he had.

"Too weird," said Tommy. "I must be dreaming."

"Woof!" agreed Nept.

Tommy pulled out his sketchpad and looked around for landmarks. He made a quick map of the area and jotted down some notes about his strange experience. Suddenly, he felt very tired. "Nept, boy, let's go home. I need some time to think," said Tommy wearily.

Nept wagged his tail and gave Tommy an affectionate nudge in a homeward direction.

It was spring break for Tommy, but his mom still had to work, so she'd left him a note on the kitchen table:

Tommy,

I hope you remembered that I have to work late tonight at the hospital. Your dinner is in the fridge. Just warm it up a bit when you get hungry. Call me at work if you need me, and if you get too lonely, you're welcome to go over to Jeanie's. I asked her to check in on you this afternoon. I hope your spring break is giving you and Nept a chance to go on some amazing adventures, honey! Stay safe. I'll see you in the morning.

    Love,

    Mom

If she only knew, thought Tommy.

Tommy spent the late afternoon and early evening trying to sort out the events of the day. By nine o'clock, he could hardly keep his eyes open. He often walked over to spend the night with Jeanie when his mom was working late, but he was far too tired to make the twenty-minute walk to his aunt's house. He gave his mother a quick call to tell her goodnight and let her know he wasn't going to Jeanie's house, then headed to his room. He was asleep before his head hit the pillow.

Several hours later, Nept woke Tommy, barking away at something in the forest.

"Not again," said Tommy sleepily. He rolled out of bed with a yawn and looked out into the night.

Nept was going crazy, barking and scratching at the window.

"Wait...where's that light coming from?" asked Tommy. He opened the window wider and listened. "Nept, hush! I'm trying to hear," scolded Tommy.

The animals were calling from all over the forest in a spine-chilling night chorus, and there was an odd sound coming from the direction of the light.

"Wow, Nept. Let's get out there!" said Tommy excitedly. He dressed quickly, tripping as he hopped on one leg to pull on his boot.

Nept, true to his breed name, retrieved the flashlight with his mouth and carried it to Tommy.

"Good work, boy," said Tommy, taking the

light from him before they hurried out the door.

Fike had been taking a slow, zigzagging course, capturing animals as he went. His sights were now set on a family of river otters, but the slippery little critters were proving to be a difficult catch.

Sensing that they were in danger, the mother and her pups tried to reach the safety of their den on the side of the riverbank. They were fast swimmers and instantly switched directions, avoiding the transport light wherever Fike shined it.

Fike became increasingly annoyed, for the creatures seemed to be experts at dodging his aim.

While Fike played his little game of cat-and-mouse with the otters, Tommy and Nept were approaching rapidly. As the scene came into view, Tommy couldn't believe his eyes. Above the river loomed the largest flying craft he'd ever seen. His first glimpse at an alien spaceship left him breathless and trembling. There was no mistaking it for anything else. It was, most definitely, an unidentified flying object.

Tommy watched the beam of light from the ship glide over the water surface and heard the otters calling out in shrill voices as they darted

swiftly to escape it. Tommy squeezed his fists together tightly, trying to stay calm, and quickly
added up the evidence in his head: *There was that
bizarre gathering of the animals this morning, and Red
Doe and Fawn were missing. Next was that mysterious
pool where we saw the reflection of our missing friends,
and now this. What...oh!* Suddenly, Tommy had a
flash of understanding. *The alien ship is capturing the
forest animals!*

From his place on the riverbank, Nept barked
encouragement to the otters. "Dive! Dive and
swim!" he instructed, unaware that Fike could easily trace their movements below the surface of the
water.

Tommy, on the other hand, assumed the river
water would be no match for advanced alien technology. "Nept, they need to get under cover! Run
that way, boy." Tommy pointed up river where a
line of trees hung far out over the bank. "Try and
get them to follow you."

"C'mon! This way!" Nept barked at the otters,
and several swam after him.

Tommy turned on his heels and ran to call to an
otter baby who'd been separated from the rest of

her family.

Recognizing Tommy's voice as a friendly and familiar one, a lover of the forest and its inhabitants, the frightened pup darted up the exposed bank toward him for safety.

"No! Go back!" Tommy yelled.

But it was too late. The next thing Tommy knew, he was standing in a flood of blinding light. He tried to run but couldn't move a muscle. His skin began to tingle from head to foot, and he had the funny feeling that he was floating.

A moment later, he opened his eyes to find himself still standing on the riverbank, or at least what he thought was the same riverbank. He wasn't sure what, but something about it seemed different, and the arrangement wasn't quite right. He scanned his surroundings in confusion.

The otter pup was standing at his feet, yelping in distress.

Tommy squatted down and sheltered the frightened baby underneath him, and the little otter peeked out from between Tommy's knees. "Where are we, little girl?" Tommy whispered.

Fike stood behind the force field, shocked. *What*

have I done? I accidentally captured a human! It was the last thing he wanted to do. He knew he'd have to return the boy, but he wasn't sure how to correct his terrible blunder. *Maybe the boy doesn't realize he's actually on a spaceship,* Fike thought. *But surely he now knows something about my activities here on Earth.* These troublesome thoughts raced through Fike's mind. *I know! I'll erase his memory of the ship so he can't tell anyone else about it, then I'll return him. Yes, that's what I'll have to do.*

Fike appeared out of nowhere in front of a bewildered Tommy. He'd seen pictures of humans, but to see one in the flesh was entirely different. Blinking, each stood perfectly still, mesmerized by the other's appearance.

Fike was tall and thin. He looked almost human, but his hair and coloring were quite out of the ordinary and amazing. His almond-shaped eyes were greenish blue and translucent, like deep pools in the Caribbean Sea. His pupils were vertical black slits, ever changing in length and width. His skin was golden orange, except for a greenish-blue, almost teal stripe that began at the top of his tall forehead, narrowed to a V between his eyes, then followed the outline of his triangular nose. It was interrupted only by Fike's delicate mouth before it continued down his chin. His hair was a deeper shade of teal, cut short, several inches above his shoulders. His chest was bare other than a band of thick, silky hair that grew from the base of his shoulders and circled his entire upper body. His only clothing was a pair of black leggings and a wide, elaborately decorated belt covered with an array of impressive gadgets. His slender, golden-orange feet were long and bare.

"Hello," said the alien at last. "I am Commander Fike, from Planet Arcturus. You are on the spaceship *Arc*. I am here on a mission to find animals that will be relocated to my planet, and I'm afraid you have accidentally been captured with the water creature. I'm very sorry, and I promise to return you safely to your home," continued Fike.

Stunned to silence, Tommy couldn't find his voice.

"Follow me please," said Fike.

Tommy didn't move because he simply couldn't. He was paralyzed, glued to the floor, and his mind was reeling. His mother had always told him to remember to breathe deeply when he was in a stressful situation, and only after he inhaled and exhaled several times was he able to speak again. "But how...how do you know my language?" asked Tommy.

"I studied Earth culture before I arrived here. You have been observed before," replied Fike. "The interpreter can translate many Earth languages, English among them." He motioned to a device he wore on his belt.

"I see," said Tommy in a mechanical voice while staring at the foreign apparatus. He was in shock and didn't understand any of it, and he wondered for a moment if he was really dreaming or if he'd slipped in the forest and hit his head too hard on a rock. "Somebody pinch me," he muttered under his breath.

"I can assure you no one will cause you harm here, not even a pinch," Fike said, not quite under-standing Tommy's remark. "This way please," the commander said, motioning for him to follow.

Tommy's eyes dropped to his web-footed friend. "What about the pup?" he asked.

"She'll be all right here, in the enclosure," answered Fike.

"No she won't! She's all alone and frightened," Tommy objected.

Fike hesitated briefly and looked down at the trembling creature. "Very well. She may accompany you."

"Follow me, girl," instructed Tommy.

Eager not to be left behind, Little Pup's long body stretched after Tommy like an expanding accordion.

A portal appeared in the force field, revealing that the river scene wasn't real. Tommy stepped through the opening feeling as though he was entering another dimension. He looked around him in amazement. It was something like being behind the scenes at the zoo or a public aquarium like the one his mother had taken him to visit in Atlanta, and he tried to take it all in.

He followed Fike along a corridor that weaved through the containment areas. On either side of the passageway, he saw life-sized terrariums with interiors that closely resembled the woods below. They contained many forest animals. At Red Doe's enclosure, he stopped abruptly and called out to her. "Red Doe! Red Doe!"

But the deer didn't look up.

"She can't see or hear you," said Fike. "She's behind a one-way invisible wall, of sorts. We can see her but she can't see us."

"But she's okay?" asked Tommy.

"Yes, yes. They're all just fine," said Fike, "and we've made sure they have everything they need."

Tommy paused and looked all around him. He appeared to be in a giant dome. The ceiling was clear, and the stars could be seen through a thin grid of fluorescent green lines. The floor beneath him was comprised of a grid of iridescent colors. The whole place hummed in soft, slow, harmonious tones, punctuated by moments of silence. "Why are you doing this?" asked Tommy. "I mean, why are you taking the animals?"

Fike didn't answer and only said, "This way please." He then led Tommy out of the maze of holding areas and down a long, narrow tunnel. "I will explain when we reach the command center."

"Fine," Tommy said, "when we reach the command center."

CHAPTER 5

The Arc

At the riverside, the silence was dreadful. The spacecraft and the bright circle of light had disappeared. Even the distressed otter family was momentarily stunned into silence.

The sky was velvet black, with a million stars twinkling brightly. A warm breeze rustled through the leaves.

Nept stared up at the sky, not sure what to do without his stolen master. He ran aimlessly back and forth, occasionally standing on his hind feet, as if he hoped to sprout wings and fly.

There was a shrill cry as the mother otter realized that one of her pups was missing. "Nept, I can't find Little Pup! I think she disappeared in the light!" yowled Mother Otter.

"Tommy has disappeared too," said Nept.

"What can we do?" The poor otter asked frantically, then trembled when she saw the helpless expression on Nept's face.

"I-I don't know," Nept said with a stutter. "I suppose it's up to Tommy now. He's gonna have to find a way back and bring Little Pup with him."

"And I'm sure he will," said Raccoon reassuringly. He had arrived on the scene just in time to see what had happened. "Tommy is a very resourceful boy and smart too. Why, I bet he's already working on a plan to get himself and that little otter back here. Those aliens made a big mistake when they took Tommy. You just wait and see!" Raccoon rambled on, trying to be encouraging.

Big Owl flew down to a low branch and spoke softly to his friends. "Sorry, Nept and Mother Otter. I know you feel awful right now, as we all do, but we have to believe they will get back home. It's wise to think positive."

Little Pup's siblings, along with many other forest animals, slowly joined the worried and bewildered group on the riverbank. There seemed to be nothing to do but watch the sky, wait, and hope.

Onboard the *Arc*, Tommy began to feel more and more like himself, and his natural curiosity and sense of adventure overshadowed his fear. Fike didn't seem too threatening, and Tommy was exceedingly curious about him. "Commander Fike, how come they haven't discovered you yet?"

"Who?"

"Um...the military, astronomers, the FBI, or

somebody? There are all these movies and books about aliens and UFOs, but nobody seems to have any solid proof."

"Humans don't recognize matter that vibrates at certain frequencies. The particles of this ship move so fast that your kind are unaware of it. The only time the ship is exposed and vulnerable to the human eye is if I'm using the transport light. I must match the frequency of the ship with the energy of the living matter I'm transporting, in order to keep them safe," Fike explained.

"Wow," said Tommy. "That's incredible. How does the beam work? Did it leave behind that pool where I found the reflections of Red Doe and Fawn? You know, that glistening white stuff? Was that from when you captured them?" asked Tommy.

Fike was amused. He hadn't expected the Earthling to be so inquisitive, especially one so young. "Have you heard of antimatter?"

"Not really," said Tommy.

"Hmm. Well, the pool was caused by negative energy, something akin to the way photographs are made from film negatives," explained Fike.

"I know movies are sometimes called films, but I have a digital camera," said Tommy. "I don't know anything about how film works."

"That's right. Surely your technology has advanced somewhat, as ours has over the years. Let me try to explain. Old-style cameras use film to capture light energy called photons. It is the energy in each photon of light that causes a change to the photographic detectors that are coated on the film. The film is exposed to photons when the camera lens opens, and the film captures a negative image of what was there. Do you understand thus far?"

"I think so," Tommy said, nodding, though he wasn't sure if he really understood or not. He was beginning to think Commander Fike sounded too much like a science teacher.

"In a similar way, when matter is removed from space, it imprints an image of itself on its surroundings. The image dissolves quickly with the movement of, say, wind or water."

"Or when disturbed by a living creature?" questioned Tommy.

Fike smiled. "Yes, like yourself."

"You know, you'd make an awesome guest at

the school science fair. Why, I'd go all the way to the state competition with you in my booth. I don't guess you'd consider that, would you?"

Fike laughed, realizing their worlds weren't that much different after all; he had participated in science fairs as a boy himself. He also realized that he hadn't laughed in ages, and for the first time, he was glad he'd mistakenly brought the curious boy onboard. Appearances aside, Tommy reminded him of himself as a child. "I don't think that will be possible," said Fike. "No one is supposed to know I am here, including you, my friend."

They had been walking for ages, with no end to the dark labyrinth in sight. Tommy's hand brushed the wall, and he was startled to realize it was soft and spongy. When he removed his hand, he saw that he'd left behind an imprint.

Suddenly, seemingly out of nowhere, a disembodied voice cited information: "Alien life form? Carbon structure, humanoid. Gender? Male. Approximate age? Ten Earth years. Physical state? Balanced. Emotional state? Excited—"

"Computer, discontinue analysis please," ordered Fike.

"Whoa! That thing was talking about me!" exclaimed Tommy excitedly. "That's amazing! How can it know all those things? And where does the voice come from?"

Fike chuckled. "You ask too many questions."

Finally, a little while later, they entered the command center by passing through a portal that instantly adjusted for their size and height.

"Oh man, this is unbelievable," said Tommy as he looked around him. When Little Pup made a chuckling sound at his feet for attention, Tommy bent over and scooped her up into his arms.

What he saw around him was beyond anything he could have imagined: Alien markings moved like writing across invisible screens; three-dimensional, lifelike models of Earth and the other planets of the solar system slowly circled the sun; and images of planets and galaxies Tommy had never dreamt of appeared and disappeared on the control center walls. Everything appeared to be three dimensional, even the alien writing.

Fike walked ahead, passing through the floating models of space as though they weren't there.

"Huh? I thought this was all...I thought everything was solid," said Tommy. He couldn't help but dodge the images as he walked past them.

The room was a large one, and along one of the outside walls, dozens of fluorescent cones grew out of the floor like stalagmites rising from the bottom of a cave.

"What are those for?" asked Tommy.

"They supply energy to the ship," replied Fike.

Tommy gasped as he caught sight of another alien. She looked like a feminine version of Fike. Her skin and hair color were the same, though she didn't have that weird ring of hair around her shoulders. She was wearing a long, silver shift dress with a wide, ornate collar around her neck, as elaborate as Fike's belt. She approached them with respect and gave Tommy the traditional Arcturian greeting of holding her hands together, palms up in front of her, for Tommy to touch.

Fike demonstrated the expected response to the greeting by touching her fingertips with his, then nodded for Tommy to do the same.

She was ice cold, which caught Tommy off guard.

"Computer, meet Tommy," said Fike. "Tommy,

meet Computer."

"Wait, she's…this lady's a computer?" asked Tommy, looking at Fike in disbelief. "Are you a computer too?"

"No," Fike said, laughing again. "I am most certainly a real, physical, living being like you. Computer is the virtual embodiment of the operating system of this ship. She is a projection, like a hologram, only solid," Fike explained.

Tommy scrutinized her carefully from head to toe and decided he wasn't sure he could tell the difference.

"Computer, please take our guests to my quarters."

Computer led the way into a sparsely furnished room. "Here you go," she said. "My research suggests you will be comfortable here."

Tommy looked out of the window, which offered a spectacular view. "Earth!" he said with a gasp. He'd seen pictures of Earth in his science books and on the Internet, but none of them could have compared to looking at it with his own eyes from space. They were really only a few miles above the planet, but Tommy could easily see the curve of Earth's sphere. "It's so…wonderful," he said, having trouble finding adequate words to describe the sight before him. "It looks so, so…small and blue and…beautiful." He felt a lump in his throat, which completely surprised him.

Fike had quietly entered the room. "I understand your feelings. Earth is your home. Would you like to sit down?" he asked, remembering his own reaction to seeing Earth for the first time.

"Your place of origin is here," Computer said, pointing to a southeastern place on the North American continent.

"Talk about geography!" Tommy said shaking his head. He took a seat across from Fike and forced his attention on his alien host. He spoke awkwardly at first, not knowing where to begin. "Uh, you know, Nept must be going crazy right now, and I bet Mother Otter is too—not to mention the hysterical fit my mom will have if she doesn't find me safe in bed when she gets home. You know how mothers can be, I'm sure." Tommy paused a moment before continuing. He wasn't afraid, and he wanted to make that clear by speaking boldly. "Commander Fike, I'm not really sure why you want our animals for your own planet, but it's wrong to remove them from their homes. You have to return them to the forest on Earth, where they were born and where they belong, with their friends and families."

"Who is Nept?" asked Fike.

"He's my dog and best friend," answered Tommy proudly. "He's a black Lab."

"You are best friends with an animal?" asked Fike, as if he'd never heard anything so absurd.

"Yes," said Tommy. "I've had him since he was a puppy, and we do everything together. Oh, and Mother Otter is Little Pup's mom, in case you and Computer haven't figured that part out." He stroked the baby otter's back. "She must be very worried."

"Curious," replied Fike. "I had no idea humans could feel such a strong attachment to animals or even that one animal could feel bonded to another."

"Of course they can!" said Tommy. "What planet are you from anyway?" Tommy was kidding, of course, but Fike and Computer only thought he had a short memory.

"As I told you, I am from Actur—"

"Lighten up, Mr. Spaceman. It was only a joke."

"Oh," said Fike. "Please allow me to explain. Arcturus is a barren planet, not like Earth. It was once alive with many wild and beautiful places, but over time, the Arcturians changed the environment, and all that was lost. Now we seek to rebuild our planet's natural areas. Therefore, we have re-created a wonderful wilderness preserve. It's a forest like yours, except it's not populated with animals. My mission is to capture animals and bring them to my planet."

"What happened to the animals that lived on your planet? Surely there used to be some," asked Tommy.

"When their habitats disappeared, so did they," Fike replied sadly, with a touch of shame in his voice. "That was a bit before my time, but it still grieves me greatly."

"Sounds to me like you expect *us* to pay for *your* mistakes," Tommy said boldly. "That isn't fair to our animals. Besides, those forest creatures are my friends, and they have families in the forest who will miss them. Their homes and everything they need are in the woods where they grew up, and they depend on each other. They don't belong to Arcturus. They belong to Earth and to the forest they came from."

"You are very wise for your age," said Fike, seriously considering Tommy's words. "However, not all your people are so wise. Take another look out the viewing window. I want to show you something rather distressing," said Fike.

Tommy hadn't noticed the nearly invisible grid that sectioned off the view.

Computer gave the window coordinates, and the northern half of South America appeared. She continued entering numbers, zooming in on the continent below.

"Do you know this place?" asked Fike.

"Sure. It's South America," answered Tommy.

"The largest rainforest on your planet is located there."

"Yep, the Amazon Jungle," Tommy said in recognition.

"Correct," said Fike, impressed with Tommy's knowledge of geography.

As they spoke, the screen zoomed in closer.

Tommy saw large areas of lush, dark green on the viewing window.

"The dark green is the rainforest," explained Fike. "Over half of Earth's known plant and animal species dwell in those forests, yet rainforests cover only a small part of the Earth."

The view zoomed closer to the surface, and Tommy could see brown and orange patches. He also saw dark gray areas of smoke rising from a number of places. "What's with the forest fires?" he asked, a bit disturbed by the sight.

"Those were purposely set by humans to clear the rainforest for farming,"

"What!? But why?" asked Tommy. "Don't they already have enough land to farm on?"

Fike sighed. "The rainforest is a rare treasure, much like the natural areas we used to have on Arcturus, but like Arcturians, humans fail to see the unique beauty and value in it. I'm afraid your people are making a horrible mistake that may be impossible to correct." He gave a nod to Computer.

The scene shifted, and the shape of North America could be seen. Computer zeroed in on Tommy's part of the world, entering coordinates at an amazing rate. She brought the familiar forest into ever-closer view and zoomed in on a section that Tommy didn't recognize. It was like looking at the forest through a powerful telescope, down to a clear image of a single leave on a single tree.

"Is that the woods near my home?" Tommy guessed.

"Yes," answered Fike.

Tommy's expression turned to horror when he realized that even parts of that forest—of *his* beloved forest—had been destroyed. Trees lay in a jumble on the ground, and huge, work machines, like angry metal dinosaurs waited there, eager to haul the chopped-down trees away. "But I've never seen that before! Where is this place exactly?" asked Tommy with alarm.

"It's at the far north edge of the forest, not many miles from where we found you tonight," replied Fike. "It has obviously been selected for clearing."

"No way," said Tommy in disbelief. "This can't be happening! It can't be true! Surely they wouldn't—"

"I'm sorry, Tommy," said Fike, "but it's very,

very true and very, very unfortunate."

"Why are they doing it? How much are they planning to clear?"

"I'm afraid even Computer doesn't know the answer to that, but I can tell you from experience that once it starts, it seldom stops until it's too late."

"You're right, Commander. The whole forest could be in danger! I've gotta get back and warn the animals. We have to stop this!" cried Tommy. "Commander Fike, please! I need to go home!"

CHAPTER 6

~~~~~

The Truth

Nept gazed lazily up at the stars, worn out by worry and helplessness. Judging by the position of the constellations, he thought it was early morning, sometime after midnight. He sighed deeply and shook his head in despair. *Tommy's mom will be getting home soon,* Nept thought to himself. *She'll be even more worried than I am, and she'll have no idea where he went.* For once, he was glad he couldn't speak to humans directly. After all, there was really no good way to explain to a mother that an alien spacecraft had abducted her son.

Most of Nept's forest friends were now dozing on the bank, all except the worried and heartbroken Mother Otter, who was sheltering her two remaining pups in the hollow of a nearby tree. Like Nept, her eyes were fixed on the sky, and she was waiting for a miracle, hoping her Little Pup would come home.

Raccoon approached Nept quietly. "You all right, pal?" he asked.

"Yeah," Nept responded in a bit of a whimper. "Why are we waiting here, Raccoon?"

Raccoon stared at the shimmering white substance that now covered the ground where Tommy and Little Pup had last been seen. No one had disturbed the site, so the mirror image of Tommy and Little Pup were still visible in the moonlight; that only made everyone miss them all the more. "I guess because this is as close to them as we can be right now," said Raccoon.

Nept smiled at him. "Guess you're right, buddy."

Just then, a bright, focused light shone down from above. Sparkling, rainbow-colored lights began to dance just above the spot where Tommy and Little Pup had been snatched. *The Arc* had returned and was hovering above them, emitting that strange humming sound they'd all come to loathe.

Nept sprang to his feet and instinctively began to bark.

The sparkling lights increased in number and intensity until the colors merged into a glimmering human silhouette. There were several blinding flashes, but when the light suddenly vanished, it left Tommy standing there in its place.

Nept let out a jubilant combination of barks, whines, and whimpers and bounded to Tommy's side. He nearly knocked him over trying to lick his face.

"Down, boy! Down! Geesh, Nept, take it easy, would ya?" Tommy said, "I'm not the only one who's glad to be home." Tommy leaned down to let Little Pup slide out of his arms.

Mother Otter ran to her baby, chittering, "Thank you! Oh, thank you!" over and over again, even though she knew Tommy couldn't necessarily understand her words.

The other animals were ecstatic to see Tommy and Little Pup and surrounded them with a chorus of excited greetings. They were full of questions, but they knew they'd have to wait for the answers.

Tommy glanced at his watch and saw that it was well after midnight. He looked around to get his bearings and wondered if he'd only been sleepwalking. He wished wholeheartedly that were true, for everything he had experienced that evening seemed too bizarre to be real. The one thing he was sure of was that it wasn't the time or the place to think too much about it. He knew his mother would be returning home from work any minute, and he didn't want to worry her. "Come on, Nept. We gotta get home!" Tommy yelled.

Tommy and Nept made it to their house just as headlights appeared in the driveway. Tommy threw open his bedroom window, and he and Nept climbed quickly inside. He could hear his mom entering the front door and putting down her purse and keys, so he quickly stripped off his clothes and boots, threw on his pajamas, and dived between the sheets while Nept curled up on the rug beside his bed and pretended to be asleep.

Seconds later, the bedroom door opened, and Mrs. Williams entered. She picked up the clothes from the floor, shook her head at how muddy and sweaty they were. *My little adventurer,* she thought. Then she pulled Tommy's cover over his shoulder, assuming he was far away in Dreamland. When she heard a *thump-thump-thump,* she knew Nept was wagging a greeting. "Hello, boy," she whispered. "Sorry to wake you." She left the room a moment later, satisfied that all was well, then closed the door behind her.

Tommy was exhausted, but he couldn't possibly fall asleep, for there was too much on his mind. "Nept, you wouldn't believe what I saw," he said to the dog. "I was on the spaceship and met the alien. It was amazing! His name is Fike, and he's so awesome! I saw Red Doe and Fawn, and they're doing okay, but Fike wants to take them to his planet, Arcturus, to live. Oh, Nept, there's so much I wanna tell you. I wish you could really understand me so we could have a conversation like other best friends do," said Tommy, turning on his back to stare at the ceiling.

Nept whined and rolled his eyes. He understood every word his young master said, and he could talk just fine. It was Tommy who couldn't understand. The language barrier was just as frustrating for man's best friend as it was for the young man.

Tommy continued to speak, unaware that his comment had annoyed Nept. "Cool as it all was, Nept, I found out something awful. Somebody's cutting down the forest! The alien showed me from the ship, but I won't believe it till I've seen it for myself, in case it was some trick of their fancy computers and gadgets."

Nept was shocked to hear such news. "Rrrrr... woof-woof!" Nept had so many questions, but Tommy had gone silent, lost in his thoughts. *How frustrating!* thought Nept. *He can understand an alien and not me, his constant companion!*

Onboard *The Arc*, Fike was still quite disturbed by his encounter with Tommy. He carefully lifted his craft and maneuvered her into orbit. The Earth sun rose before him, then set at the rear as he entered the dark side of the planet. He felt torn inside. *Is the Earthling boy right? Perhaps it is wrong to take these animals away from their natural homes.* Fike thought about things deeply for a moment and began to see that it was all quite connected. The web of life on his planet had been changed forever, destroyed by the progress of one species, effectively wiping out all the others. He wondered what the consequences of his current actions might be. What had happened on Arcturus was about to happen on Earth, and it would affect that planet in a bad way as well, even if it was on a smaller scale.

Something else concerned Fike too. *The boy claims animals have thoughts and feelings similar to humans and make strong bonds with each other. Why, he even has a canine for a best friend! If this is true,* thought Fike, *do I have a right to destroy those bonds? To interfere in those relationships and hurt those feel-*

ings? He did not wish to cause pain or injury in any way, even emotionally. The last thing Fike had expected was to find himself in a moral dilemma, and he felt somewhat annoyed at Tommy for stirring up that distasteful conflict inside him. Clearly, many wild places on Earth were being threatened, and not all Earthlings were as passionate as Tommy about protecting the planet's wildlife and natural places.

The sun rose before him once more, and Fike looked down at the beautiful planet and felt a great tenderness and empathy for Earth and her inhabitants. "What might have happened if someone from another world had visited Arcturus before we abandoned and destroyed our wild places, if they had seen the glorious planet Oma had so adored?" Fike asked himself. "Could our wildlife possibly have been saved? It's not too late for Earth. Many wild gardens remain." As Fike considered these things, his mind turned once more to Tommy.

He was unable to erase the memory of the boy who so reminded him of himself. Fike knew from the very moment that he met him that Tommy was special, and he could not bear to alter the memory of his new friend any more than he could pretend that their encounter had not influenced his own thoughts and feelings. He thought about his beloved Oma, the only family he'd ever known, and he recalled her wonderful stories, the ones she told him time and time again about the bygone days, when the world was so much more beautiful. Although Tommy was an Earthling, Fike felt a kinship with him. It broke his heart to think that Tommy would have to tell his grandchildren stories someday of the wild creatures he had known—that he would have only stories to tell because those creatures would all be gone.

Fike took a deep breath and let it out. One way or another, he knew he had to find a solution to the dilemma, and a plan began to form in his mind.

Sunlight was streaming through Tommy's bedroom window. It was late morning, and the smell of bacon and coffee filled the air. Tommy rubbed the sleep from his eyes and suddenly remembered his strange adventure. He bolted straight up in his bed. *Did it really happen? Was I really on a spaceship, talking with an alien named Fike, looking down on Earth's bare spots?* Tommy's feelings of amazement turned to alarm as he remembered Fike's determination to take away his animal friends, and he was even more upset when he recalled that the forest was being cut down. "I have to do something!" he shouted out loud.

Nept was having an enjoyable dream about chasing a squirrel when Raccoon suddenly entered his reverie, demanding his attention. He woke to hear Raccoon calling to him excitedly from somewhere outside. Tommy was so distracted by his thoughts that he barely noticed the fuss Raccoon was making, but Nept rose and leaned out the window to listen. It must have been good news, because Nept began to bark and wag his tail.

"What's going on, Nept?" asked Tommy.

Nept responded by tugging on Tommy's pajama sleeve.

"Nept, I don't think I can take any more excitement today," Tommy said wearily.

Nept was persistent, though, and gurgled a friendly growl, then pulled harder.

"Okay, okay! I'm up already," said Tommy.

While he dressed, Nept did his best to wait patiently. *It'd be so much easier if humans only had to wear their fur every day,* he thought. When he saw that Tommy almost had his shoes on, he ran out the bedroom door, bolted down the hallway and out the kitchen, stopping only to push the screen door open with his nose.

"Good morning, Nept," said Tommy's mom to the fleeting black shadow passing through her kitchen. Mrs. Williams shook her head in resigned amusement; her son and his dog lived in a world she couldn't even imagine, and they were always on the go. *They don't even need coffee,* she thought with a yawn. As she turned back to her frying pan, she heard the screen door slam again. "Tommy!" she yelled.

"I'll be right back, Mom."

"Hold it right there, mister," said Mrs. Williams. "You're not going anywhere till you've had your breakfast."

"But, Mom, I'm not even hungry and—" Tommy tried to protest, but his mother stopped him with a hand in the air and nodded toward the kitchen chair.

"You heard me, young man," she said firmly.

"Oh, all right," said Tommy.

Nept didn't have to go far before he found Raccoon and some other friends at the edge of the forest. "Red Doe and Fawn? You're back!" exclaimed Nept. He ran to his friends and greeted them with a round of his famous sloppy licks. "What happened? Are you both okay?" asked Nept. "Tommy said the alien wanted to take you back to his planet. How did you get home?" Nept asked, very curious about their experience.

"We're fine but tired. It's a long story, and to tell the truth, I...well, I don't know exactly what happened," answered Red Doe.

"Let me tell him, Doe," Raccoon pleaded excitedly. "The alien sent them home this morning, and I found them at the same grassy knoll where they'd disappeared. I heard that weird humming noise again and went to investigate. They saw the alien! Doe says his skin is as orange as a pumpkin and his hair as bright green as spring grass!"

"Teal," corrected Red Doe.

"Oh, yeah. That's right. Teal. Anyway, Red Doe said he kept them in some sort of invisible cage, but it looked like a forest, like home. When she saw the alien, she was scared, but he turned out to be okay.

He explained that he was sending them back and even apologized for frightening them. Doe even thought he looked a little sad. The next thing they knew, they were back, though she wasn't sure where she was until she saw me. Isn't that right, Red Doe?"

"Yes, Raccoon. Like I said, it's a long story."

"I can't wait for Tommy to see you," said Nept. "He needs some cheering up. What happened to him anyway? I thought he was right behind me."

Tommy, meanwhile, was stuck at the table in his mother's kitchen.

"What have you and Nept been up to lately?" she asked as she filled a glass with orange juice for him.

The color of the juice reminded Tommy of Fike's skin, and his forkful of eggs stopped midair. "Uh...well, we lost track of some of the familiar animals that live in the forest," he said.

"Really? Did they finally show up?" she asked.

"Not exactly, but we have a pretty good idea where we can find them."

"I hope so. I know how much you love all the woodland creatures," said Mrs. Williams.

"Yeah, they mean a lot to me...and to our whole world." Tommy gathered his courage before speaking again. "Hey, Mom, have you heard anything about the forest being cleared?"

There was a long pause as his mother thought for a moment. She answered casually, with as much honesty as she could bear, and the strange tone in her voice made Tommy's heart pound harder. "I did hear that the Bradleys are selling some timber. I'm sure they can use the money."

"And just how many trees do they plan to cut down, Mom?" asked Tommy.

"I'm not sure, son. I guess it's up to them, since the trees are on their property," answered Mrs. Williams before she took a sip of coffee.

"Mom, how can you be so calm about this?" Tommy asked. Tommy had never known his mother to be so insensitive. *Doesn't she realize what the forest means to me and to all the animals that live there? How can she just sit there like that, drinking her coffee and doing nothing to stop the Bradleys?*

"Tommy, the land belongs to the Bradleys, so it's within their rights to chop and sell the timber. Besides, there are lots of ways to harvest trees. You don't know how they're planning to go about it."

"What does it matter?" Tommy said angrily.

"Well, they might be using partial or selective cutting. From what I've heard, that leaves much of the forest unharmed, and some people even re-plant. Things may not be as bad as you think."

"It's worse than I even knew, Mom! They're going in there with these huge machines, ripping it all up. They don't care about the trees or the forest or the animals. I bet they'll cut down every tree in the forest! Tommy shouted.

"Honey, calm down, before you choke on your bacon. I know the Heimlich maneuver, but I'd prefer not to have to use it at the breakfast table," she said, trying to make light of the situation.

Tommy didn't say another word. He just abandoned his meal and headed out the door, holding back the tears.

"Tommy, wait!" his mother called after him, but Tommy kept going; he had to see what was really happening to the forest.

Nept returned home, eager to find Tommy and take him to see Red Doe and Fawn. When Mrs. Williams let him in, he ran through the house, searching every room for his master.

"He's not here, Nept. I'm afraid I upset him," said Tommy's mom. "I just didn't know how to tell him about the timber being cut."

So it's true! thought Nept. Outside, a soft rain had started to fall, but he paid it no mind and headed out the door so he could track Tommy's scent but lost it as the rain fell harder. He shook himself off and headed back home, feeling defeated; it was useless trying to pick up Tommy's scent in the downpour, even with his miraculous nose. *Besides, Mrs. Williams looked like she could use some company,* he thought.

CHAPTER 7
~~~~

Strange Visitor

When Tommy returned home that afternoon, he was the gloomiest Nept had ever seen him. His mom had tried to talk to him, but he wasn't ready to listen, and Nept felt bad for them both. Apparently, what Tommy had seen in the woods had only upset him more.

The morning rain eventually stopped, and the sun came out to dry everything up and warm the Earth once again. Nept decided to walk to the river, hoping to find a cool breeze. It seemed to Nept that things had been spinning out of control lately, and he felt the need for a little timeout. He sighed and plopped down on the riverbank, feeling tired and helpless. "After all, what can a mere canine do to change the course of things?" he asked himself. His head started to nod, and before long, he was fast asleep, basking in the warmth of the sun and the soft murmur of the flowing water.

"Nept? Hey, Nept, wake up!"

Nept opened his sleepy eyes to see Beaver's face right in front of him. "Yikes!" he cried out. "Beaver? Don't sneak up on me like that, ya hear? You nearly scared me to death!"

"Shh! Be quiet," said Beaver, holding his paw

up to his lips. "Hush, or he'll hear you."

Nept shook his head, trying to wake himself up, and stared at Beaver, slightly annoyed to have been disturbed from his peaceful nap. "What?" asked Nept irritably. "Who'll hear me?"

"He's here," said Beaver.

"Who?" asked Nept again, angling his head to the side.

"The spaceman," whispered Beaver. "The orange and teal spaceman is here!"

Nept's eyes grew large, and he sat up quickly. "Where?" he asked, darting his eyes from side to side.

"This way," said Beaver. "Follow me." Beaver slid into the water and started swimming away from shore.

Nept hesitated, hoping Beaver wasn't trying to play some practical joke on him, then quietly entered the cool water and swam after him.

Nept had not been the only one in search of some rest and relaxation that day. Fike had also been feeling a bit burned out from his animal-snatching mission, and he had decided to look for Tommy and offer his help, but first he just wanted a chance to look around. He had never set foot on Earth before, and the forest went far beyond his expectations. For Fike, it was like visiting a wonderland from his boyhood dreams.

What surprised him the most were the various smells. He was overwhelmed by the environmentally rich aromas of moist, healthy earth, fresh air, bountiful water, and the endless variety of plants. Fike walked around sniffing everything, trying to make sense of it all, and everything smelled wild and amazing.

As he walked along the riverbank, he spotted a school of minnows swimming by, and his curiosity led him straight into the river. He had never waded in a natural body of water before. The forest around him was intriguing enough, but the water was a whole other world!

The cold current streamed around his legs, and the algae-covered rocks felt slippery under his bare feet. The water itself seemed to be alive. Occasionally, he saw a fish swimming below the sparkling surface.

He was startled when he disturbed a snake that was sunning itself on the rocks. It slithered into the river and swam away, holding its head several inches above the water like a periscope, leaving a curvy line of pretty geometric patterns in its wake. *Incredible! Absolutely incredible,* thought Fike.

Rocks glittered beneath the water surface, enticing Fike to collect a few as souvenirs. Leaning over, he lost his balance, and he fell in with a huge splash. He was glad he'd left his control belt on the riverbank, so all of his gadgets would stay safe and dry.

Nept and Beaver couldn't help but chuckle.

"Will you look at that?" said Nept.

"He's so…colorful!" marveled Beaver out loud.

"No kidding!"

"Wait…aren't dogs colorblind?" commented Beaver.

"Not completely, but I thought beavers were."

Beaver chuckled. "Not me," he said.

"I've gotta admit, he does have some very distinct markings, and that hair around his shoulders is interesting. I don't need color to see that," remarked Nept.

"What do you think he's up to?" asked Beaver. "Doing a little fishing?"

"I don't know, but look over there. He left something lying on the bank."

"Looks like some sort of fancy strap," said Beaver.

"I bet he wears it around his waist, like the one Tommy wears to keep his pants up. Looks important, don't you think?" Nept said as a naughty, nosy idea dawned on him.

The two had been spying on Fike from the cover of a narrow island situated midway across the river and overgrown with trees and vines.

"What if I could get close enough to grab it? I could snatch the belt before he gets out of the river, just so we can have a peek at it."

"Are you crazy?" asked Beaver. "What if he zaps us with those strange alien eyes or decides to take us on a tour of his spaceship?"

"Beaver, who cares if he comes from outer space? He doesn't look all that frightening to me, sort of like an odd-looking human. Besides, I'm willing to risk it. I bet he's powerless without that shiny belt. He can't even keep his balance in the water."

"Oh all right. What do we do?" asked Beaver.

"Here's the plan. You swim out where he can see you and flap your tail a few times. Make a big show of it to keep his attention. Meanwhile, I'll circle around behind him and grab the belt," said Nept.

"Okay, but I hope you know what you're doing," said Beaver.

"Trust me, it'll be fine," Nept said with a wink.

"Give me a bit of a head start before you start your little act," said Nept, slipping into the water on the opposite side of the island. He swam in a wide circle, taking care to stay out of sight.

Beaver waited until he saw Nept coming around the end of the island. "Here goes," he said, then swam within a few yards of Fike and started an ardent performance of water slapping, splashing, and gymnastics.

Fike was delighted by Beaver's sudden appearance, captivated by the flat-tailed creature's incredible display. "What an odd animal," he said aloud. "I suppose he doesn't like uninvited guests," he uttered, guessing Beaver's antics were meant as a warning because he'd trespassed in the creature's territory. "I mean you no harm, water creature," said Fike. He began to slowly back up.

In an effort to hold the orange being's attention, Beaver became even more animated, to no avail.

In the next instant, the alien turned to climb the bank, just in time to see Nept snatch his belt. *"Nejha! Ba zhu, Ba zhu!"* shouted Fike.

Nept didn't understand the language, of course, but he had a pretty good idea of what he was saying. He grabbed the belt with his strong retriever jaws and was ready to take off with it, but he hadn't counted on its being so heavy. He only managed to move it from its resting place before he lost his grip; it felt like an iron weight. *Wow! If this guy wears that around, he must be made of steel,* thought Nept.

Fike had clumsily waddled out of the water and was now only a few feet away.

Nept decided then and there that he wouldn't give up his prize without a fight. *If I can somehow get that belt to Tommy, it might give us some advantage over the alien,* he reasoned. "Woof! Woof! Grrr...woof!" Nept assumed his most threatening posture: back hair raised, ears back, and teeth bared menacingly. He barked and growled ferociously, hoping Fike wouldn't test his nerve.

"*Ba zhu, Ba zhu!*" ordered Fike.

"Beaver, do something," barked Nept. "Help me!"

"How?" asked Beaver.

Fike suddenly froze. He stared at the translator on his belt, then at Nept. "But you…you can talk!" said Fike in amazement.

Nept looked up at Fike in surprise. "What?"

"I-I'm entirely able to understand you. I can't believe this. It must be the interpreter on my belt. I-I had no idea that animals could…that you—"

"That we what?" asked Nept. "That we have brains, like you?"

"That animals can talk. This is truly remarkable!" said Fike.

"I can understand you too," said Nept.

"May I have my control belt back?"

"Not just yet," warned Nept. "I think Tommy should have a look at it first."

"Tommy? Oh! You must be Neptune, his canine friend that he told me about," said Fike. "Do you know where Tommy is? I wish to talk to him as well."

"What about?" asked Nept, surprised.

"Your mast...er, uh, friend has helped me see things quite differently, things about our worlds. I want to help him save the forest," answered Fike.

"Why would you do that?" asked Nept suspiciously. "You don't even live here."

"Tommy and I talked when he was aboard my ship. I learned much from him about your planet and the animals here, many things I didn't know or understand before and some things even Computer doesn't know. He opened my eyes and made me see that it's wrong for me take the animals from this place. I also had some things to show him, the most important being that this beautiful forest is in danger of being destroyed. He was very upset, and I believe he intends to do something to stop it. I want to help him with that mission if I can," explained Fike.

Can I really trust this strange alien? Nept wondered. He had returned Tommy and Little Pup unharmed, and the return of Red Doe and Fawn sure made it seem as if Fike had had a change of heart. On top of that, neither Tommy nor Red Doe had made him out to be menacing. *I really have no choice but to risk it,* thought Nept. *He may be the only chance we have to save the forest.* "Okay. I'll take you to him."

"Good. Now may I have my belt please?" Fike asked, holding his hand out.

Nept approached Fike cautiously and dropped the heavy belt at his feet.

"Thank you," Fike said as he picked up the belt and fastened it around his waist. "Oh! Please excuse my rudeness in not properly introducing myself. My name is Fike, and I am the commander who pilots *The Arc,* from the Planet Arcturus."

"Glad to meet you," said Nept, wagging his tail just a little. "As you know, I am Neptune, Nept for short."

Beaver, who was still in the river, cleared his throat loudly. "Ahem!"

"Oh…sorry," said Nept. "That's Beaver in the water there."

"Hello, Beaver," said Fike. "I very much admire your most interesting tail."

Beaver looked at Fike strangely and said nothing. He refused to move an inch closer, in spite of the alien's polite introduction and compliment.

"It's all right, Beaver. He's going to help Tommy out," Nept barked.

"Are you sure that's a good idea?" asked Beaver.

"Don't worry," said Nept. "I'll catch you later."

"Okay, but be careful," warned Beaver, looking sideways at Fike. "And you better be nice, mister, or I'll slap you with this most interesting tail!" he said, then scurried off before Fike could respond.

Nept led the way through the forest, back to the house where he and Tommy lived. He was well aware that many eyes were on them, and he could hear a steady, soft hum of inquisitive chatter whenever they were seen together. Fike was agile on land and seemed to spring lightly from one step to the next, as if his feet were made of rubber or had springs on the bottom. Between his surefootedness and Nept's fourfootedness, they arrived at Tommy's house in no time.

"Wait here. I don't think it would be a good idea for Mrs. Williams to see you, so I'll see if I can get Tommy to follow me," said Nept.

"Take this with you," said Fike. He removed the control belt from around his waist. "I think

Tommy will recognize it."

Nept nodded and took the belt in his mouth and headed inside. He struggled a bit to pull the screen door open with his paw, as the heavy belt made things difficult, but he finally managed to slip into the kitchen. All was quiet inside the house, and he padded softly to Tommy's room, where he found his master writing in his journal. Nept whined softly to get Tommy's attention.

"Hey, boy. Where've you been?" asked Tommy. "Sorry I took off without you this morning. I was pretty upset. I guess I should apologize to Mom too," Tommy said without even glancing up from his desk.

Nept dropped the heavy belt on the floor with a clunk to get Tommy's attention.

"What you got there, fella?" Tommy asked.

Nept picked the belt up again and took it to him.

"Hey! Where did you get this?" asked Tommy, recognizing the alien design on the buckle.

"From Commander Fike," answered Nept.

Tommy glanced up at Nept, thought a moment, then looked all around the room to see where the voice was coming from. He looked back at Nept and gave a little laugh, shaking his head in confusion. "You know, either I'm going crazy, or somebody's gotta be playing a joke on me," said Tommy. "For a moment there, I thought I heard you talk to me." Tommy shook his head again looking down at the floor.

"You did," said Nept, enjoying every moment of it.

Tommy froze, then slowly looked up to stare at Nept. "You…you can talk?"

"Of course," Nept said, "but only in Labrador and English."

"But you…uh, that's not possible. I mean, how could…oh man! It has to be the belt, right? Fike's translator works for animals too?"

"You got it," said Nept.

Tommy paused to gather his wits. Ever since Fike had flown that ship into their forest, a whole new array of things had become suddenly possible, including talking dogs. "Is Fike here? Is he on Earth?" asked Tommy.

"Yes. In fact, he wants to talk to you. Come with me." Nept headed for the door, wagging his tail.

Fike was hiding behind an old shed in the back of Tommy's yard.

Tommy stopped short when he rounded the corner of the old building and saw Fike standing there, looking totally out of place, an alien in his own back yard. Tommy was speechless for a moment. He glanced down at the belt he was holding, then slowly handed it to Fike. "What are you doing here?" he finally asked, when he could find his voice again. "Didn't come for the science fair, I hope, 'cause we're on spring break," he said with a smile.

"I have come to help you," said Fike. "I returned your friends, the deer and her offspring, this morning, along with all the other animals I had taken."

"You did?"

"Yes. Since we spoke, I have thought long and hard about your world and all who live here, animal and human," said Fike. "As you said, it is very wrong for me to take the forest animals away from their homes."

As if to prove that Fike was telling the truth,

Red Doe and Fawn emerged from the woods, right on cue.

"Red Doe, Fawn! Welcome home, you two!" Tommy approached them and lovingly stroked Red Doe's soft neck while Fawn nibbled at his hand in search of treats. "Thank you, Commander Fike. I needed some good news today."

"You do not have to address me so formerly, Tommy. Fike is fine." Fike paused briefly before continuing, "I think of you as a friend, and I want to help you save the forest."

"Really?" asked Tommy.

"Absolutely," replied Fike, smiling.

"But what about your mission? What about Arcturus?"

"We can discuss that later. Right now, I want to tell you about my plan to save the trees in your forest. On *The Arc*, I have something very special. It came from my planet, but I believe it can help yours."

"Okay," Tommy agreed, astonished by the sudden turn of events.

Fike's plan was rather simple, and there were no guarantees that it would work. In fact, much would depend on the wisdom of the Earthlings. They agreed, though, that they'd put the plan into motion and then see how things developed.

"We can watch safely from *The Arc*," Fike suggested.

"Really?" Tommy said excitedly. "Talk about a bird's-eye view!"

"It's fine with me, as long as it will not cause anyone to worry about your whereabouts," said Fike. "We must not alarm your mother. You know how mothers can be," he said with a coy smile.

"Awesome!" exclaimed Tommy.

"If all goes well, the forest will be saved from further clearing. I will meet you at dawn by the river, home of the otters," said Fike.

"Excellent," said Tommy. "Fike, how do you wish someone good luck in your language?"

"*Ahzshum boharr.*"

"Well, in that case, *ahzshum boharr*!" repeated Tommy.

CHAPTER 8

~~~~

The Plan

The logging crew arrived at dawn with the bird song of early morning. They started up their saws and revved up the engines of their clearing equipment. The big trees shivered and quaked as the ravenous tree harvesters cut them down one by one. The smell of gasoline and diesel fuel filled the air, along with swirls of sawdust from freshly cut timber.

Two distressed crows called out high above their nest, "Caw-caw!" as if begging them to stop, but the saws continued to buzz.

A workman was clearing a path with his bulldozer when it suddenly quit. "Man, can't I ever catch a break?" he complained to himself as he tried to restart the engine, without success. As he jumped down from his seat to check out the stubborn machine, something unusual caught his eye. He'd never seen anything quite like it and simply had to walk over for a closer look.

Growing in front of the bulldozer was what appeared to be a small tree. Its flat, round leaves were beautifully marbled in turquoise and purple. Blossoms resembling exploding fireworks adorned its branches in shades of red and gold. Its trunk was held off the ground by a multitude of sturdy roots fanning out on top of the soil like bicycle spokes. Its lovely appearance was completed by the silvery-white color of its smooth limbs and branches.

How beautiful, thought the workman. He noticed that the blossoms were wonderfully fragrant and made him feel strangely alert as he inhaled the invigorating scent.

One by one, the other machines refused to cooperate with their operators, drawing a string of angry shouts and grunts as the men dismounted them.

"Hey, Joe, what's up with the equipment?" asked a frustrated crewman.

"I-I don't have a clue, man, but get over here and take a look at this," replied the dozer operator.

"Wow. It's...odd. I haven't ever seen a plant like that before in these parts. What do ya think it is?"

"I'm not sure, but I think we should get the foreman over here to take a look at it."

A few minutes later, the crew supervisor arrived. "Joe, what's the holdup?" he asked, obviously irritated that he'd been bothered and that trees were not crashing down around him at a steady enough pace.

"I don't know what's goin' on with the equipment, Boss, but look at this thing I found. I ain't never seen nothing like it."

The supervisor sighed heavily, then bent over to study the unique tree carefully for a moment. "Hmm," he said as he stood, then scratched his scruffy chin as if he wasn't sure what to do. He noticed glittery drops of liquid collecting in the center of a blossom. He cautiously approached and slowly dipped his finger in the sweet nectar and touched it to his tongue. His sleeves were rolled up, revealing nasty briar scratches on his lower arms. He became aware of a light tingling sensation on the surface of his skin and before his eyes, in a matter of seconds, all the nicks and cuts were healed, as though they had never been there. He stared at his arms in disbelief for a moment, then dipped his finger in the nectar again and rubbed it on a wart that had long bothered him; instantly, the wart disappeared, leaving behind only smooth skin. He licked his dry, cracked lips and gave a command. "Joe, you stay right here and don't let anyone near this tree—or whatever it is."

With that, the supervisor jumped in his truck

and picked up his cell phone to make a call. When the landowner picked up, he said, "Hey, Mr. Bradley. This is Jim Kouple, out at the timber worksite. Uh, we've discovered somethin' pretty amazing out here, and I think you oughtta come down here and take a look before we keep choppin'."

It took some convincing, but Mr. Bradley finally agreed to stop by and examine their strange discovery. When he did, he was persuaded to rub a drop of the tree's nectar on a bruised nail that had been causing him a lot of pain. He watched with wide eyes as the nail was immediately healed. "Holy mackerel!" exclaimed Mr. Bradley. "That beats anything I've ever seen!"

It didn't take long before Mr. Bradley was making some calls himself, and his first one was to the head of the Botany Department at a nearby university. "Hello. Is this Professor Brown?" he asked.

"Yes. How may I help you?"

"My name is George Bradley, and I was wondering if you'd be willing to check out a very unusual tree we just discovered on my property. We've never seen anything like it. Would you be interested?"

"That depends, Mr. Bradley. I'm a busy man, but tell me about this tree of yours."

"Well, sir, I would, but I think you'll believe it better if you see it for yourself."

Reluctantly, the professor agreed to stop by, just in case there was something to the story. He was quite impressed by what he saw and excited to share the discovery with his colleagues and students.

After that, the news spread like wildfire. Within a few days, the area was full of botanists, research scientists, conservationists, reporters, and even the county sheriff.

The story made the local news in no time, then national news, then international news. Specialists from all over the world camped nearby, just outside Tommy's beloved woodland, hoping to get a look at the odd little plant. The timber operations were put on hold as specialists tried to understand the power of the tree and where it had come from.

Tommy, Nept, and Fike couldn't believe it. The plan seemed to be working better than they could have ever expected. Days passed, and they only hoped the discovery of the tree would stop anyone from wanting to tear down the forests for timber or anything else.

After a while, the Bradleys finally announced that they would halt the clearing of the forest so scientists could thoroughly investigate the phenomenal discovery and the circumstances surrounding it.

Cheers erupted onboard *The Arc*, as Tommy, Nept, and Fike realized that Fike's wonderful little Arcturian tree, replanted on Earth, had successfully rescued the woodlands from destruction.

"Fike, you did it! You've saved the forest!" announced Tommy, pulling his orange and hairy alien friend into a big hug.

Fike was surprised by Tommy's gesture, for he'd never been embraced so enthusiastically before. Not sure how else to react, he only chuckled and accepted the hug.

Nept barked and wagged his tail triumphantly.

"This calls for a celebration!" Fike excused himself and returned with a rare Arcturian treat that was eaten on only the most special of occasions.

"What is it?" asked Tommy as he suspiciously eyed the strange food.

"The fruit of the keebie plant. It grows in our forest. Take a bite," prompted Fike.

"Mmm! It's so good," said Tommy. "It tastes like Mom's key lime pie, only better...and neither of you better tell her I said that."

"I agree," Nept said enthusiastically.

"What? Since when does Mom give you pie instead of dog food?" asked Tommy.

Nept dropped his head and looked up at Tommy with guilty eyes, and Tommy and Fike couldn't help but laugh at him.

"Oh, Nept," said Tommy. "It's all right. I won't tell Mom you're a pie thief!"

"Keebie grows wild and was almost lost to us, along with our wild animals," said Fike, glancing down at the floor with a sad and shameful look on his face.

"Fike, I can't thank you enough for helping me save my forest," said Tommy, "but I feel horrible that you will have to tell your superiors that you failed at your mission. What about Arcturus and the forest there? Will you get in trouble? Won't the Arcturian people be very disappointed after they put all that hard work into re-creating your forests?"

"You ask too many questions, Tommy Williams," teased Fike. "Don't worry about me. I'll search for places where wild animals are in terrible danger, here and on other planets. Perhaps I can make it my new mission to save those whose habitats have already been destroyed, animals that have nowhere else to go and will die if not rescued. Either that, or I'll return home and let my people know that we must learn to live without wildlife. I hope that won't be the case, because animals do so much to brighten the world, but whatever decision I make, I will always put the welfare of the animals first. That's a lesson I've humbly learned from you, Tommy. In fact, I've learned much since I first came here, and I only have you to thank. My Oma would have been proud to know you, just as I am. Thank you."

"Your Oma?"

"My grandmother," Fike said, his eyes gleaming as he remembered her. "She was a very special person indeed…and she always told me I asked too many questions too."

"Well, you're most welcome, Commander Fike."

"Before we part, I have something for you." Fike

reached for a handsomely decorated pouch and pulled from it a beautiful, round crystal, the perfect size to fit in the palm of his hand.

"What is it?" asked Tommy.

"Something for you and Nept to remember me by. Treasure it, and in time you will discover what it is," said Fike.

Tommy nodded. As usual, he had a million questions, but it was a puzzle Fike seemed to think Tommy should solve on his own.

"I think your forest will be fine now," Fike said with a smile. "It's time for you to leave my ship and for me to be on my way."

Tommy's eyes filled with tears. He couldn't express his gratitude or his sadness enough in saying goodbye to his most unusual friend.

Fike responded to Tommy's expression with tenderness. "I will miss you also," he said, and placed a warm hand on Tommy's shoulder. "Take care of your forest." Then Fike bent down to scratch Nept's ears affectionately. "And you, loyal one, take care of your master."

"Of course," Nept barked into the interpreter. "That's my job."

"Well, then I guess this is goodbye," said Fike. He boldly held out his hand to shake Tommy's.

"*Ahzshum boharr*," said Tommy.

"Yes, good luck," chimed in Nept.

"And good luck to you in all that you do," said Fike. "I will never forget either of you." Fike paused for a moment to take one last look at his friends. He smiled at them warmly, then transported them safely to the forest below. *The Arc* dipped to one side in a final goodbye, then disappeared. For Tommy and Nept, it seemed all to soon for their adventure to end.

In the days that followed, the marvelous tree was found to be growing at several other sites in the forest. It was proven to have miraculous healing properties, and people called it, The Mirabel Tree, which stems from the Latin word for "wondrous." Its mysterious appearance baffled everyone, for it was unlike any other plant found on Earth.

Eventually, the Bradley family sold their property to a conservationist group. The Mirabel Tree was given protected status and studied for its healing powers. To protect it, the entire woodland became a plant and wildlife sanctuary.

Because Tommy had firsthand knowledge of the forest, perhaps more than anyone, he found himself cast into the role of a resident expert. He felt honored to be consulted by specialists from all over the world. He told everyone about Fike and Planet Arcturus and explained that the tree was a gift from them. He also reminded them that forests all over the Earth contain native plants and animals with secrets every bit as valuable, just as Fike had told him to say. Not everyone believed his fantastic story, but that mattered little to Tommy. He knew the truth, and it had forever changed him.

Weeks later, Tommy and Nept were lying on a blanket out on their front lawn. It was a clear August night, and there were almost as many lightning bugs flashing as stars twinkling in the sky. It was so clear and dark that they could see the Milky Way.

"Look, Nept! There's Aquila, the eagle. The Greeks thought of Aquila as the messenger of the Gods. And there's Hercules. Do you see him up there?" asked Tommy, pointing.

"Woof!" answered Nept.

"I sure wish I could still understand you," said Tommy, "like when we had the translating device."

He rubbed the top of Nept's head.

They watched quietly for a while, gazing at the stars that seemed to suggest just how infinite space had to be.

Finally, Tommy said, "Do you think he'll ever come back?"

Nept knew Tommy was talking about Fike, and he whined softly, not knowing the answer to the question.

"Yeah, I miss him too," said Tommy. "I wish I'd had more time to get to know him. "

"Woof!" Nept agreed.

Just then, a shooting star streaked across the sky, followed by another. "Wow! Did you see that, Nept?"

The big Lab wagged his tail.

"Maybe that was Fike saying hello. We can think of it that way, and every time we see a shooting star, we'll be reminded of our alien friend and his wonderful ship."

Nept and Tommy looked dreamily into the heavens. Tommy had pitched his tent, and they planned to stay out all night. Soon school would start again, and the lazy summer days and nights would end. But for the time being, Tommy and Nept were free to enjoy all the wonders of nature and each other's company.

Tommy reached into his pocket and pulled out the pouch Fike had given him. He let the ball roll out into his hand and rubbed his thumb over the surface. It made a clicking sound, and a soft, white light began to glow from within. "Hey, Nept, what do you suppose this is?" asked Tommy.

"Greetings from Planet Arcturus," said a familiar voice.

Tommy gasped in surprise, then turned to Nept with an expression of happy discovery all over his face. "Hey! Look, boy! It's a communication device!" he exclaimed.

Nept, as shocked as Tommy was, jumped to his feet and whined in excitement.

Tommy held the ball near his face and spoke into it. "Fike, is that you?"

"Who else do you know from outer space, young man?" Fike said with a chuckle.

The End

ACKNOWLEDGMENTS

So many wonderful people helped me write and illustrate this book. Special thanks to Mark Dubowski and Annette Hall, who got me started on this journey. Thank you to my husband, Darryl Wally, and my son, Kasen Wally, for your endless patience. Thanks also to Alaä Craddock, Christine Kushner, Michelle Duncan, Jan Muscarella, Donna Gallagher, the Sronce family, my editor, Autumn Conley, and so many others who took their time to give me encouragement and helpful instruction.

ABOUT THE AUTHOR

Shirley Ann Galbrecht was born and raised in Norfolk, Virginia. She moved to North Carolina to study at Barton College, where she received a bachelor of fine arts degree. Her first job took her to the coastal town of Elizabeth City, where she worked for the North Carolina Arts Council as a resident artist. While there, the surrounding beauty of the rural farms and ocean scenery took root in her heart, and her lifelong love affair with nature flourished. Later, during her seventeen years as a graphic designer in central North Carolina, she kept her connection to the environment alive. Perhaps the greatest contribution to this has been her choice of residence in a beautiful natural area, covered in a green canopy of forests and bordering a scenic river. Shirley has always had a love for art and adventure, and that has inspired her to do such things as travel in Europe alone, land in a small plane on the top of an Alaskan glacier, sing in an a cappella group, and begin horseback riding lessons in her late fifties. She now works as a fine artist, exploring the role nature plays in our lives. She lives with her husband near Chapel Hill and is a mother and a grandmother.

23177262R00072

Made in the USA
Charleston, SC
14 October 2013